# The GARDENER AND THE VINE

## CREATED BY ANDREW McDONOUGH

ZONDERVAN.com/
AUTHORTRACKER
follow your favorite authors

ZONDERkidz

LOST SHEEP

On a wild, lonely hill, on a thin, scraggly vine, lived a branch named Basil.

Basil never visited anyone, and no one ever visited Basil, until the day the Gardener came.

The Gardener looked up and down the vine.

"Basil!" he said. "You're exactly the branch I've been searching for!"

Basil looked over his shoulder to check if there were any other branches named Basil nearby. No, the Gardener was talking to him.

"I have good news and bad news," said the Gardener. "The good news is you're going to grow lots of grapes."

"Excellent!" said Basil. "And the bad news?"

"I need to cut you off this scraggly vine."

"Oh," said Basil. "I think you've got the wrong branch."

"Trust me, Basil. I'm a good gardener."

Basil thought about the bad news.

Then, he thought about the good news.

"Okay, then," said Basil. "I'm in your hands."

So the Gardener took his clippers and...*snip!*

He placed Basil into his bag.

"This is the end!" cried Basil.

"No," said the Gardener, "this is just the beginning!"

Down the wild, lonely hill they climbed, away from the thin, scraggly vine,

across the hot, hot desert,

over the snowy mountains,

through the jungly jungle,

and into a beautiful garden.

And there stood a magnificent Vine.

"Wow!" said Basil. "Now that's a Vine."

"Basil," said the Gardener, "I have good news and bad news.
The good news is you're going to grow plenty of grapes.
The bad news is I need to cut the Vine."

"No!" said Basil. "You can't cut this magnificent Vine!"

"Trust me, Basil. I'm the Gardener."

The Gardener took his clippers and...*snip!*

He cut deep into the Vine.

Then the Gardener took Basil and placed him deep into the cut in the Vine. And the Gardener wrapped tape around and around, joining Basil and the Vine.

"This is the end!" cried Basil. "I'm going to die!"

"No," said the Gardener, "this is a new beginning. Get ready to live!"

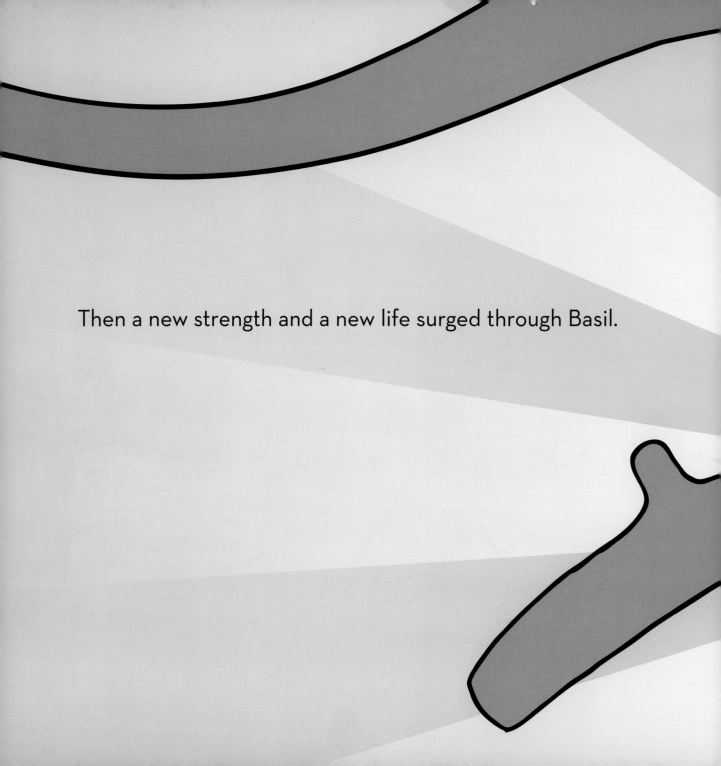

Then a new strength and a new life surged through Basil.

"Basil," said the Gardener, "meet the Vine."

"Welcome, Basil," said the Vine. "I have good news and great news. The good news is you're now a part of me."

"And the great news?" asked Basil.

"We're going to produce plenty of grapes," said the Vine.

And sure enough, that summer Basil and the Vine produced plenty of grapes, thanks to the Gardener.

# Cecil's Page

*The Gardener and the Vine* is based on the teaching of Jesus in John 15 and the grafting imagery used in Romans 11. A theme throughout the Bible is that God gathers people who are far away and embraces them into his family. Or, to put it another way, the Gardener finds a branch on a wild, scraggly plant and grafts it into his magnificent Vine. As the Bible unfolds, it tells the sobering story of how the journey into God's family comes through the suffering and death of Jesus on the cross. Apart from the cross, there is no way of sharing in the new life of Jesus. Or, in gardening terms, there is no way a wild branch can enjoy new life in the vineyard apart from cutting the Vine.

## Before the story

Begin by asking, "What is the most exciting thing that could ever happen to a branch?" "Let me tell you about the adventures of one branch."

## Read the story

## After the story

Tell your child that *The Gardener and the Vine* is actually a picture of the story of Jesus. You might like to read John 15:1,5 together and tell them the story of Jesus dying on the cross and rising again. You can tell your child that in the same way that Basil trusted the Gardener to give him new life through the Vine, we can trust God, our Father, to give us new life through Jesus. Now, that is the start of an exciting adventure! (And I know a lot about adventures.)

God's Blessings,
Cecil

# John 15:1,5 (NIV)

Jesus said to his disciples:

> I am the true vine, and my Father is the gardener...If a man remains in me and I in him, he will bear much fruit.

ZONDERKIDZ

*The Gardener and the Vine*

Copyright © 2010 Lost Sheep Resources Pty. Ltd.

Requests for information should be addressed to:

Zonderkidz, *Grand Rapids, Michigan 49530*

Library of Congress Cataloging-in-Publication Data

McDonough, Andrew (Andrew John)
　　　　The gardener and the vine /created by Andrew McDonough.
　　　　　　　p. cm. – (Cecil and friends)
　　　　Summary: Basil, a branch on a scraggly vine, learns that when we trust in God and His loving care, we become a part of the family of God. Story based on the teaching of Jesus in chapter fifteen, verse one of John's Gospel.
　　　　ISBN 978-0-310-71946-5 (softcover)
　　　　[1. Trust in God–Fiction. 2. Christian Life–Fiction. 3. Plants–Fiction.] I. Title.
PZ7.M4784456Gar 2010
[E]-dc22
　　　　　　　　　　　　　　　　　　　　　　　　　　　　　2009023102

*Author and illustrator: Andrew McDonough*
*Editor: Mary Hassinger*
*Art direction: Cindy Davis*

*Field Naturalist: Bronwyn Drew*
*Horticultural Advisor: Paul Smith*

*When reading this book outside, wear a wide-brimmed hat and sensible walking shoes.*

*Printed in China*

10 11 12 13 14 /GPC/ 10 9 8 7 6 5 4 3 2 1